THE COLOURS OF A

BY THE SAME AUTHOR

Leviathan and other poems
(Allison & Busby, 1984)

THE COLOURS OF ANCIENT DREAMS

B. C. Leale

John Calder · London
Riverrun Press · New York

First published in 1984 by John Calder (Publishers) Ltd
18 Brewer Street London W1R 4AS
and by
Riverrun Press Inc
175 Fifth Avenue New York NY 10010

Copyright © B.C. Leale 1984

ALL RIGHTS RESERVED

British Library Cataloguing in Publication Data
Leale, B.C.
   The colours of ancient dreams.
   I. Title
   821'.914   PR6062. E195
ISBN 0-7145-4037-4

Library of Congress Catalogue Card Number: 84-60505

SUBSIDISED BY THE
Arts Council
OF GREAT BRITAIN

No part of this publication may be reproduced, stored in a retrieval system, or transmitted, in any form or by any means, electronic, mechanical, photocopying, recording or otherwise, except brief extracts for the purpose of review, without prior written permission of the copyright owner and publisher.

Any paperback edition of this book whether published simultaneously with, or subsequent to, the cased edition is sold subject to the condition that it shall not, by way of trade, be lent, resold, hired out, or otherwise disposed of, without the publishers' consent, in any form of binding or cover other than that in which it is first published.

Typeset in 11pt Bembo by Gedset Limited, Cheltenham.
Printed and bound in Great Britain by Hillman Printers (Frome) Ltd, Somerset.

For Bill Swainson

ACKNOWLEDGEMENTS

Acknowledgements are due to the editors of the following periodicals and anthologies, in which certain of these poems have appeared:

Ambit, Dream Helmet, Encounter, The Fiction Magazine, Global Tapestry Journal, Jazz/Linguis, kayak, The Literary Review, Litmus, The Little Word Machine, London Review of Books, Magma, Matrix, Montana Gothic, New Poems 1977-78 (P.E.N./Hutchinson), *New Poetry 7* (Arts Council/Hutchinson), *New Writing & Writers 16* and *18* (John Calder), *Palantir, Poetry Review, Rabies, Slow Dancer, Sow's Ear, spectrum, Stand, Tuba* and *Vanishing Cab.*

"City" and "Other Worlds" appeared in a broadsheet, *Three Poems,* from The Many Press.

"Fouquet's" appeared as a Sceptre Press pamphlet.

"Offer" appeared in *The Transparent Room,* a portfolio of poems and etchings from The Starwheel Press.

CONTENTS

A leg waving to surrealists everywhere	11
A memory of twelve o'clock	12
Lautréamont paraphrased	12
At the Cabaret Voltaire, Zürich (1916)	13
Where is your headache?	14
Dada	15
For sale & wanted	15
Homage to Marcel Duchamp/Rrose Sélavy	16
Offer	18
Postcard from Mauritius	19
In the studio of Marcel Janco	20
A telegram from Magritte	20
A letter from Magritte	21
At a performance of John Cage's *Theater Piece*, Rome 1963	22
What more?	22
To savour the lake	23
In the Brazilian Highlands	24
The moustache on wheels	24
Learning the language	25
The chair	26
Useful objects to have about the house	27
Drive us back to Zahlé	28
Suspensions	29
The visit	30
A dream of the film Luis Buñuel nearly made	31
In a locked room of the château	32
A room	33
The mundanities of this life	34
The dead	35
Bridegroom	36
Ceremony	37
Night music	38
Where?	39

Scenes observed on smashing down the locked door	40
The moment	41
Mr Poe at the dinner party	42
Nostalgia	43
The phenomena of natural science	44
In the Ottoman Empire, 1892	45
Preludes to the late afternoon	46
What there is in the Gladstone bag	47
On the Isle of Wight	48
At the death of Prince Albert	49
Edwardian views	50
Fractured landscapes	51
Cameras	52
Photographers in the thirties	53
A photograph by Paul Popper	54
The invitations	55
Opus 1	56
Opus 2	57
While breathing deeply	58
At the zoological gardens	59
The piano	60
The watch	61
The murderer	62
Outside my grandfather's flat	63
Poem	64
In 19th-century Heidelberg	65
In Gothic Europe	66
For a confrontation	67
Two paintings by Munch	68
Salon	70
At half past four	71
The contents of a violin case	72
Projections	73
What has happened to the week before last?	74
Has anyone found my siesta?	75
Collecting evidence, Tokyo	76

Feminine exposures	76
Étude	77
Six ways of going off	77
From *Pure and Untouched* by Barbara Cartland	78
At the end of my garden	80
Files of pigeon bones	81
Cork	82
Taxidermist extraordinaire	83
The rabbit's mouth	84
Nocturnal	84
The Englishman's flora	85
Fouquet's	86
Aunts in a deep sleep	87
Postman	88
Memories of India	89
Ceremonies of the evening	90
Echoes from the imperial past	91
Death of a composer	92
City	93
Other worlds	94
Paris conservatory	95
In the shadow of the porch	95
Museum	96

A LEG WAVING TO SURREALISTS EVERYWHERE

Lips move excitedly breeding a silence
that breaks over paralysed knives
in a carnival of flames.

A hand goes up to a head that doesn't exist
and a thought logics there —
it has the tenacity of a thing of teeth.

The light is of pale eggshells ...
within this fragility
arms jut their angles in jackets of black.

What has happened to the thought
that removes its dentures
and attempts the sterility of a glass of smiles?

A MEMORY OF TWELVE O'CLOCK

Jacques Vaché fired his horse pistol
at the horse manure
it didn't breathe
it didn't stir
it didn't turn over & dream
it didn't utter a single
four-letter word.

LAUTRÉAMONT PARAPHRASED

Beautiful as the sizzling chance encounter on a dissecting table of a pig and a slice of bacon.

AT THE CABARET VOLTAIRE, ZÜRICH (1916)

The room is dancing with nervous frayed
toothbrushes
the piano is packed with cordite and missionary zeal.

Hiccups are cut with scissors after a heavy dew
and vulgar fractions watered and autographed
in limited editions.

Tristan Tzara announces that mathematics
is a bubbling of mushrooms from the ribs of the Eiffel Tower
and that art is a blowlamp in the grip of a pig's trotters.

WHERE IS YOUR HEADACHE?

— in a box of steam-hammers
— in a Ming vase dilled with wine

— at the foot of an abyss
  built by Doré
— in the Fabergé egg where a motorcycle
  goes off in a roar of gold

DADA

is the limitless sky
fiercely flying dodos are attempting to enter

FOR SALE & WANTED

A flock of tweezers adrift on the Sargasso Sea.
Thoughts emanating from the wood of a completely destroyed table.
The *Dreadnought* stuck between icebergs on Lake Chad.
A naked redhead at gale force 10 increasing.

HOMAGE TO MARCEL DUCHAMP/ RROSE SÉLAVY

Rose

Please do not ouch

Tired Old Man

Prune on the bed

Cowes

München

Moustached Sleepwalker

Whiskered away in the somnambulance

Le Petomane

Objet f'art

Hammer Horror Film

Hitting the head on the nail

Artistic Petrol

-ou have your (our) woo
-den floors polished with dental
manure it is enough to see glass fish hoo
-ks sink through folded con-
crete then to put newspaper grave
headlines into someone's un-
dissolved childhood. Fragments of anchored
whistles bubble out of our dullest
holly. Fossil Daimlers are driven out of the past tense of exhaust ex
-humed humour being its own dirigible

OFFER
(For Bernard J. Kelly)

Grand Metropolitan Hotels offer one-night concatenations. Tears are inclusive of surreal rail travail but dada will be adad. English breakfast consists of two prunes of withered fur, a fresh cup of boiling unstirred fur and the tenderest bicycle wheels scrambled on toast. Reduced tears for a child if accompanied by an adult head chopped off or a wise saw.

POSTCARD FROM MAURITIUS
(For Charles Thorne)

Gris-Gris (Souillac) enchants us by dashing against the rocks Robert Edward Hart, the national poet. Not far away are found wonderful spectacles in a charmed case of waves breaking over "La Nef".

IN THE STUDIO OF MARCEL JANCO

I was terrified by mice & sardines
that began to recite
slowly, majestically:

on top of the languorous cabinet
filling with a turbulent ocean
the ball of mystical horsehair.

A TELEGRAM FROM MAGRITTE

FISHMONGER OPERATED ON BY STURGEON

A LETTER FROM MAGRITTE

There is a little Indian blood in the veins of the coffee.
Yesterday I visited the date on the calendar
in a flat in a white house saccharized with religious education.
I am, at the moment, seated in front of a South American jungle
(the home of psychoanalysis) in a black, prickly, Victorian chair.
Mrs Paige arouses the anacondas. Dr Vits
paints her out with a brush stiff and staccato.
The typewriter is about 50 years of age and has
no hair. It will travel back with me to Brussels shortly.

AT A PERFORMANCE OF JOHN CAGE'S *THEATER PIECE*, ROME 1963

A dead fish is flung into the piano
euphonious notes are a red herring.

WHAT MORE?

What more do you want
with your rooms full of chinoiserie
& the maids polishing steaming cases
of horse manure?

TO SAVOUR THE LAKE

To savour the lake the wait
-er winches the table down into it
& a chair & a bottle corked with
an esteemed vine-veined nose.
It is with a consummate ape
-like swagger glasses are frisked
for a lurking dust.
Sklug is everyone's sur-
name who draws lake-logged
corks. A lady's screams are cuddled
as a dead frog-leg steps oh o
-ver the rim of her
glass.

IN THE BRAZILIAN HIGHLANDS

No one needs a taxidermist's
wrung neck on their hands
or icy impromptu glimpses
into the moods of inflammable spinsters

not even a thin tongue of smoke
nailed to the ship's mast
in a triumphant blend
of care & imagination.

THE MOUSTACHE ON WHEELS

without spare tyres or a puncture outfit
the moustache on wheels tears through rainbows forever

LEARNING THE LANGUAGE

my snake has the measles
my little cousin sloughs his skin

the submarine dived and disappeared from its clothes
the gulls were dripping beneath the waves

my fishknife travels by sea
my fishwife is of chaste silver

your wife is hot air
your teacup is filled with invectives

the door smiled suddenly
the hinges fell out of her mind

she had lovely taste
she had aunts carved into furniture

THE CHAIR

the chair doesn't need to burst out laughing
or fan itself into sweetness & light
the chair doesn't suffer a touch of the vapours
or go through life whipping itself
until the blood oozes

the chair just sits in a field of snow
quiet &
self-contained

USEFUL OBJECTS TO HAVE ABOUT THE HOUSE

Pandemonium.
Green teeth.
A ship's mast.

An elephant brush.
Piano legs.
A jocular vein.

A stiff upper lip.
An ebullient boot.
Hairy eggs.

A pouncet-box.
A box on the ears.
An imperial sausage.

DRIVE US BACK TO ZAHLÉ

Please measure my neck.
I want it for a suit.
O.K. wrap it please.

You must have time for fun.
I will show you an excellent kind.
Drive us back to Zahlé.

But the sea is rough.
Do you want me to cut it short for you?
Do you want it in the first or second floor?

Please, send me the chambermaid.
Anything forbidden?
Anything contrabanded?

SUSPENSIONS

there was the young widow in Italy
there was the crate of dates by the side of an iron boot-scraper
there was the stoned Egyptian porter with a buttonhole of belladonna
to be paid off

there was a house bulging with incunabula
there were hordes of steel spectacles
on noses of the carabinieri
hunting it down

there were tigers to be eased out
of the womb of a lily
there were banks to be robbed
when I had watered my water-pistol

there was my suit to be pressed
beneath the fountains of Rome
there were the young widow's pale buttocks still shining
through the forlorn forests of Italy

THE VISIT

At the top
of the polished stairs where
the ambassador squeaks by

with his retinue
of stick-insects
blowing their
fine-boned noses

this woman
out of Bruegel
clutching a fish

sucks its head
and rolls about
grunting and sweating
on lurching earth.

A DREAM OF THE FILM LUIS BUÑUEL NEARLY MADE

Light blossoming in corridors
of impenetrable carbon

from fossil clocks
the pale chiming of fish

a kerb encrusted suddenly
with a gold Lagonda

the announced princess wrapped in the white
hairy legs of an octopus

a table set with knives & more knives
& thickening with barbed wire

elsewhere lingerie trapped in the flow of volcanic mud
being freed by crucifixes of burnt fir.

IN A LOCKED ROOM OF THE CHÂTEAU

Our philatelist uncle
with the towering crumbling eye
of a mortician
spreads out a sparkling
fresh set
of gummy vaginas.

A ROOM

There is a room possessed
by a locked piano
a black coffin
on a silent ocean.

There is a room crackling with flames
where the women you desire
unsheathe their vulvas
beneath blankets of ash.

THE MUNDANITIES OF THIS LIFE

while a wedding cake is being shot to bits
in the mortuary
wolves are resting their breathless teeth
in a vapour of ferns

THE DEAD

The dead are being dragged away. Children are stamping in the yard shouting obscenities. The dead are being forced down under the heavy incense of flowers & pressed into the wormy earth. With pale glistening skins lovers are worming over each other. They exhale the softest obscenities. Spiky. Fragrant as flowers.

BRIDEGROOM

he sat at the table
leaning upon the ocean

with a blade of marram grass
he slit his own throat
& lapped up the radiant blood

a tree screamed into the blackness

the wedding guests drifted
beneath carpets of kelp

the mourners took up the thousand and one positions
of sexual intercourse

CEREMONY

the typewriter's drunk with thunder
& abandoned fires hissing through moist grass

the brides stand on the other side of the wall
compressed springs
clutching bouquets of mirrors

NIGHT MUSIC

sisters on bicycles
wait to ride off
through fields at night
 bulging with wheat

two sisters whose hair
will tumble dark seas
through the pale restless bodies
of men asleep

WHERE?

Where is your limousine
where is your peach melba
where is your Jamaican serving girl
with the cool & sinuous fingers

or your house come to that
built from the bricks of old mortuaries
every room with its silver tray
& drowsy revolver?

SCENES OBSERVED ON SMASHING DOWN THE LOCKED DOOR

piranhas devouring the glass
of their aquarium

a clock sizzling
in its wooden tower

a dragonfly drowning its fires
in the dark pond of a cello

THE MOMENT

it is the moment when footsteps descend
past the hydrangeas without assurance
it is the moment the postman takes shoals
of letters to the lank graveyard
& leaves them gasping for breath

it is the moment when telephone flexes
slither & hiss through dreams
& birds have been beaten back
to the horizon & burnt
off the perimeter of the earth

MR POE AT THE DINNER PARTY

He's trapped within a dark labyrinth of drink/the heart
of a death's head moth's ripped open enshrining a young
girl's pallid hand/he's scaling the sheerest wall of ice
the table's lurched up against/a column of candles flickers
in vaults of obsidian seas/his broken glass
grows a thick rime of dust/the probing eyes of owls
open up dolorous pits & forgotten corners of slowly
unwinding bones.

NOSTALGIA

A buried telephone is dragged screaming
out of the blazing emptiness of the beach.
There is nothing left of the ocean but a glass of water
its rim gripped by the teeth
of an extinct fish.

THE PHENOMENA OF NATURAL SCIENCE

Five birds blazed out of a piccolo
snow settled
on a flick-blade of lightning
a cloud poured out of the library
& resumed its place
above the black stalagmites of trees.

IN THE OTTOMAN EMPIRE, 1892

An entire temple erected by Augustus fell away carelessly
over our shoulders. Weary horse-back readers
were dropping out of the dust by the side of our vaporous faces
built solidly into the dark sanctity of the bottle.

PRELUDES TO THE LATE AFTERNOON

Carrier pigeons had failed to deliver
nests of vipers from the Côte d'Azur.
Twelve archbishops cycling out of the river
had thrown themselves in numerous pieces
over the Hurlingham lawns. Charred
skeletons of umbrellas huddled
on the edges of fire-escapes. The sabre-
toothed tiger to welcome guests by the aspidistra
was not everyone's cup of tea.

WHAT THERE IS IN THE GLADSTONE BAG

A letter from Marconi
or a cat's whisker.

A crystal ball decanting
dark voyages over the snow.

Queen Victoria's teeth
vitrified by lightning.

ON THE ISLE OF WIGHT

Osborne Bay and the Solent beyond command superb panoramic views of Prince Albert's bathroom, his bar of soap for the year 1846 and his personal sponge containing 27 magnificent holes. Set about the sky are life-size marble replicas of chimney smoke carved by Mary Thornycroft.

AT THE DEATH OF PRINCE ALBERT

The view from his well-dressed moustache remains unaltered: five white clouds and their sunlit filaments are supported on Cubitt's cast-iron beams. His razor lies baying for blood in a vase of calves-foot jelly. Nightingales continue to sing in his bodiless bath darkening the steam with a march from *Tannhäuser*.

EDWARDIAN VIEWS

on a photographer's tripod
a vase of hummingbirds

& the Taj Mahal diminished
by our cousin's bosom

FRACTURED LANDSCAPES

teeth are in the viewfinder
the photographer's head is under a black cloth
the black cloth bursts in flames to reveal
a fish in a dark wood

the viewfinder is under a lake
the lake is under a mountain
of teeth & exploding fish
in the photographer's ruined head

CAMERAS

on three legs of wood
a mouth devouring the landscape

on three legs of silver awash with sapphires
a dung beetle rolling its pellet

on three legs of ice crystals
the symphonic weight of Chartres Cathedral

on three legs of blue smoke
the confused eye of the conjurer's white rabbit

PHOTOGRAPHERS IN THE THIRTIES

They walk around Paris with light
tucked under their arms
jostled by fierce lepidopterists
& are coaxing it into their cameras
that wait on the Quai des Orfèvres.

How sad that dazzling black shadows
are all scampering away
on the backs of armadillos.

A PHOTOGRAPH BY PAUL POPPER

Brahms has dynamited the back of the piano
& is tugging a viola
out of the sepulchral blackness.

A sunlit waterfall plunges
from the edge of the keyboard
& magpies shelter beneath it with trays of opals & sapphires.

THE INVITATIONS

it wasn't as if Moiseiwitsch was keeping his bees in order
behind the hedge
or trimming his long-haired piano with garden shears
or clearing the staves each autumn of fossil ivory
but his invitations did go out
in impeccable ink
flourishing their mud & mussel-blue black
beneath the weary legs of a pier

& it wasn't as if Moiseiwitsch was failing to prise the light
in its drenching tumults of silk
from the carved Stygian Bechstein branchy with wax
of blazing baroque

OPUS 1

A Stradivarius pushes through difficult ground to flower
its finest textures
but the case of a Steinway is driftwood on the beach —
a net of piano wire searches the ocean bed
for a shoal of elephant tusks.

OPUS 2

The eggshell gradually cracked in which he was sitting
punching the keyboard as if it were a set of teeth
in a black open-lidded skull.

When Tchaikovsky stepped down to shake him by the leathered fist
no one was there & nothing seemed to exist
but spidery vapour & the smell of cathedral stones.

WHILE BREATHING DEEPLY

think of a piano
think of a sponge inside the piano
& a sponge-diver descending through blue-green depths

think of the bubbles rising out of the piano
& breaking in the auditorium
crisp as glass

AT THE ZOOLOGICAL GARDENS

I left the tiger's teeth bloodless
in the tiger's mouth.

I withdrew my hand from that cavity of hot air
that could have grown clamorous with crushed bone.

I trotted it back to my ferny & delicate flat
& let it swoon over the keys of the pianoforte.

Where would Mozart be with his encyclopaedias
of profound fritillaried sound

without these ivory fillets
cut from dun shambling mammalian mountains?

THE PIANO

the piano
with its teeth puncturing a throat
swells with blood

with dark humours
that seethe through forests
& the echoing vaults of abandoned castles

THE WATCH

The watch is blown up
with sticks of dynamite
on alternate Sundays

or cut into succulent
pieces & thrown
to the birds on the Avenue Mozart

who reassemble its golds & enamels
in the shape of a cloud
& set it ticking across the sky.

THE MURDERER

the murderer
discharges into dark oceans
bottles of poison

the murderer sculpts his graceful way
through suave ballrooms
leaving little heaps of broken smiles

the murderer runs through rainy streets
his trilby dripping
with blood

OUTSIDE MY GRANDFATHER'S FLAT

the stairs were dilapidated as music
profound holes around which
the entire orchestra sat
in concentrations of silence

& the postman ascended
brushing through
withheld glissandi of diamonds
clutching a long slippery envelope constructed of bones
aimed at someone's throat

POEM

greenflies trickle through air emeralds rain incessantly
on the grave of Carl Fabergé
a coal splits open a fern unfolds its bronze
rubescent with rubies
the Czar shakes ivory dice
splattered with black
gold typewriters soar from crags with talons clattering "murder"
bellowing elephants lift padded tusks
in resonant silence
moonlight is drenched with sonatas

IN 19TH-CENTURY HEIDELBERG

a vulture's brain is being lifted
from the doctor's surgery
& folded carefully into a waiting ambulance

horse dealers are rubbing their fingers
lovingly along the veneered flanks
of sheet lightning

the murderer's axe surfaces gasping for blood
a museum attendant guards it
with his death

IN GOTHIC EUROPE

in Gothic Europe
behind hushed curtains
in crumbling churches
knifed organists
weak hands
on keyboards summoning
thin music
out of the silence
crash
into black ravines

FOR A CONFRONTATION

a gravel drive through the pines
a house barely lifting itself
beyond the enervated
fountains

a doorknocker with a voice of thunder
a spiral staircase pushing the room up
into icy latitudes

TWO PAINTINGS BY MUNCH

The Scream

A jetty
spiders out of the sea.
The sky's blood-vessels break.

A sound from the unbuilt future
rises with whining shrillness —
its hot needle presses
through the base of a solitary head.

Hands valve down onto ears. Sound
earths in nerves of terror.

The Dance of Life
1
It's a dance by the night sea.
There's the red-eyed feverishness of approach
that keeps its
inhibited distance.
There are hands that touch and become
needed chasms.

Dresses move sinuous and slow. The sea
hisses.

2
Her beauty feels the finest
touches of erasure.
No man cleaves the air
with requests or demands.
Her hands tighten in a spinstering grip
over thighs that are lost.

SALON

Cigarillos cast espaliers of smoke
studded with jewels of aromatic wit.
Legs weak & tedious spindle down
& snake away from pontil marks on pools
full of loquacious grape.
Legs treadle into a cinereous dawn.

AT HALF PAST FOUR

at half past four the chandelier will explode
& its crystals be found
in abandoned lead-mines

at half past four the Chevrolet will drive
into a binding snowdrift
& the passengers climb down
into blue lakes ringed with towering organ-pipes

at half past four the cat will go searching through the green
                                                    chambers
of a whale's brain

at half past four the door that has never opened
will burst into plumage & the eternal flames of song

THE CONTENTS OF A VIOLIN CASE

Rocks. Feathers.
First carbon drafts of flight.
Hydrofoils planing an ocean.
Crystal clocks.

A billiard table's
liquid ivory. Tower blocks
soaked in flamingo
erased by night. Light-
ning's discharged crumpled gold.

PROJECTIONS

An arm drifts white as steam from a letter-box.
A cannon fires one hundred and seventy-nine bloodied
hands that ooze out of its hot mouth.
A collection of fine eyes is carried on trays of elm
into tropical rain forests
(the desert smoky with the negatives of abandoned heads).
Kropotkin studies *The Military Use of Insects* but the order Isoptera
dissolves its dream of world domination.
A piano lies heavily lidded.
Its light will bring about the rediscovery of fountains
at the touch of a Mozart.

WHAT HAS HAPPENED TO THE WEEK BEFORE LAST?

It is lying on a sheet of ice
among billiard-balls
slowly
disintegrating
recorded on tape
recorded on film
& on matt surfaces
silently
handed round
on the ocean floor.

It is an oblong space
on the other side
of many thickets of sleep
littered with bullets
& the carcasses
of smouldering kisses.

HAS ANYONE FOUND MY SIESTA?

Is it under the afternoon
    or a little
    to the side
full of oranges
full of diamonds
    on the hilts of daggers
weighed down by minute
    typography
    & abandoned hangars
full of dust
full of the rusting bones
    of disused trains
full of a piano concerto
    an elephant
    is extracting his teeth from?

COLLECTING EVIDENCE, TOKYO

Five policemen chase
smoke rings round a revolver
with butterfly nets.

FEMININE EXPOSURES

The nates are out in shining ardour.

ÉTUDE

A baboon
releases the moon
with the ecstasy a ghost has when it might walk
through fields of chalk.

SIX WAYS OF GOING OFF

goes off his head buried in a newspaper

FROM *PURE AND UNTOUCHED* BY BARBARA CARTLAND

The Duke walked through the shrubs holding his
big Balls and Receptions right on the edge of the sea.

Anoushka looked up at him, her eyes no longer
propped against the side of the balcony.

Their kiss took a long time while the Duke
paid some of his tailor's bills.

Then she smiled at him as she opened the door of
his brains, his intuition driven by his coachman down the Champs
                                                                    Élysées.

The Duke's lips twisted behind her like the tail-feathers
of an angry chair she had recently vacated.

Anoushka put her small hand on
the bitterness in his voice arranged in one wing of the Palace.

The Duke gave a sharp laugh, and it was
in the mirror over the mantelpiece and was watching what he was
doing.

She carried in her hand an envelope which contained
the years fallen into disrepair.

AT THE END OF MY GARDEN

I am writing a history of Iceland's baroque opera
my toes languidly lobstering in numerous hot springs
the snow maidens smoking footnotes addenda & corrigenda
out of the ripe doddery vines
& fat ladies & gents in 18th-century togs
pranging out of the trees deploying a language recherché
— ah well
I must turn in for one & a half puffs at my meerschaum
& feed the skeleton clock with some gibbering seed.

FILES OF PIGEON BONES

I was searching among my files of pigeon bones
& there is was:
the photograph of the *Île de France*
sinking slowly
beneath its freight of bouquets of roses
with Dietrich & Garbo waving
from forlorn portholes.

I left my top hat & bow tie with the harbour police
& jumped into the dark waters knowing
that when Dietrich & Garbo had hauled me aboard
we would start the futile search
for my lost files of rusting pigeon bones.

CORK
(For Marita O'Donovan)

city of skyscrapers powered with querulous candles
city flooded with juniper roots
city of museums swelling
      with tethered zeppelins
city where a single abstemious wine
      is a red shape lapping at the lips

city foliaceous with books
      creaking open
      onto shadowy gardens of laudanum
city of cormorants diving
      into a butcher's wall of meat

TAXIDERMIST EXTRAORDINAIRE

the taxidermist is stuffing bulbs
with electric light
and soldering them to wire perches

every time he switches them on
a bone explodes inside a bird's head
and a hearse gallops off in a cloud of flowers

THE RABBIT'S MOUTH

out of the rabbit's
mouth floats a top hat

out of the top hat
a magician springs

NOCTURNAL
(For Steve Wheatley)

Who's drunk my
dreamy
musical
glass teeth in
the toothglass?

THE ENGLISHMAN'S FLORA

a garden
for cheetahs to mince in
on crazy pavings
among Peruvian lilies

a machine-gun
adorns the aubrietia
the Chinese lanterns are stolen
by headless green-eyed birds

the lake's dark liquid lid
is opening to disclose
a mastodon's towering bones
buried in red valerian

FOUQUET'S

1
Tweezerings of iced
volcanoes. Tumbril whirls. Delicate
lit spindles. At Fouquet's you replace your glass
excessively (a gramme of strength
gone from you). It's charged with a pale deluge
of sipped grape. The imagination's Venice
crusted in snow.
The Piazza brimming with an unspilt light.
The sky's gondola riding a harbour of stars.

You step into the street drilled by its
rough lexical strata.

2
Where's Fouquet's? Nine-tenths
beleaguered by snow. By black skies
battened down. A mooring place for the frail legs
of pencilled moustaches.
A smoky cabinet of liquor & books.
Your place reserved. Your paper & ink
set up. A bottle of Vouvray awaits
your demented entrance. A glass asylum
for the expanding fictions of Chapter 1. The un-
finished.

AUNTS IN A DEEP SLEEP

aunts in a deep sleep
have inherited the house
with its subterranean alcoholic haze
with its locked rooms at night
wildly aglow
with fountains of underclothes

aunts in a deep sleep
have inherited the lake
damp as a morgue
where the last of the rufous uncles
abruptly vanished
with a little wave of his glass

POSTMAN

he arrives with a sackful of blackness
his descending footsteps
cast in the rungs
of despair

he arrives with a blue ocean
he arrives with a white liner's
distant &
wistful smoke

MEMORIES OF INDIA

typists crouched in the jungle
dipping their fingers
into quick
liquid metal

tigers sniffing
the machines
extracting thin ribbons
of blood

CEREMONIES OF THE EVENING

flowers are burying their colours
servants are dragging the last rays of sunlight
from the monkey-puzzle tree

it is time to blow the bassoon
it is time to set free the flute
from the drums & their cavernous thunder

ECHOES FROM THE IMPERIAL PAST

sunlight roars
off the edges of the Sheraton table

the spider goes up in flames
on the snows of the Himalayas

the valet sits polishing his master's
tusks beneath the Indian Ocean

DEATH OF A COMPOSER

the conservatoire accepts your head
of febrile marble
& the polished somnolent
fruits of autumn

the damp black carapaces
of grand pianos
abandoned on distant hills
in a gauze of grasses

CITY

Swelling suddenly
above the fret
of buildings

a cloud of ochreous
smoke
swathed in sunlight

alchemizing our lives
with a strange
joy.

OTHER WORLDS

the piano
feathers down
upon a city asleep

the dreamers
are leaving caves
of velutinous fire

& float over ivory roads
flanked by the black-
lacquered ilexes

PARIS CONSERVATORY

flowering in a glass-
enclosed room
delicate
exotic
pianos

IN THE SHADOW OF THE PORCH

There is a dazzling absence
above the chessboard
now that the peacock has flown
into it own reflection
& the sky in its heavy gilt frame
has been carried down
into the earth.

MUSEUM

You have stepped out of the museum
with its butterflies sawn in half
& its blonde chrysalids that spring up
quite unscathed.

There were photographs of yourself
in a cabinet of curiosities
& in states of anxiety Latin names
breathing out of the wall.

You have left the museum with its violent
thunderstorms stored in vaults
& its blinds drawn over the fading
colours of ancient dreams.